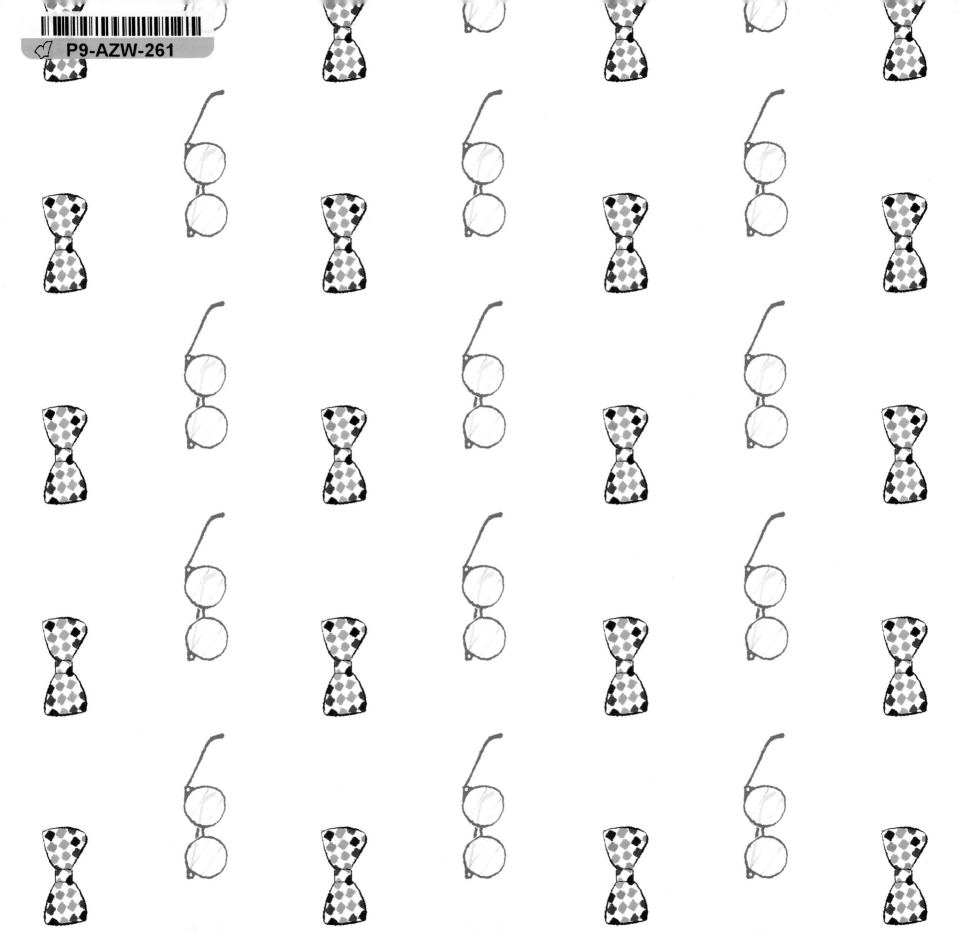
P9-AZW-261

Last Week Tonight with John Oliver presents

A Day in the Life of

MARLON BUNDO

Written by Marlon Bundo with Jill Twiss

Illustrated by EG Keller

CHRONICLE BOOKS
SAN FRANCISCO

Hello. My name is Marlon Bundo, and I am a bunny.

I live with Mom, Grandma, and Grampa in an old, stuffy house on the grounds of the U.S. Naval Observatory. That's because my Grampa is the Vice President. His name is Mike Pence.

But this story isn't going to be about him, because he isn't very fun. This story is about me, because I'm very, very fun.

This is the story of my Very Special Day.

My Very Special Day started out like every other day.

I woke up all alone.

Then I ate a fine bunny-breakfast all alone,

while I watched the news . . . all alone.

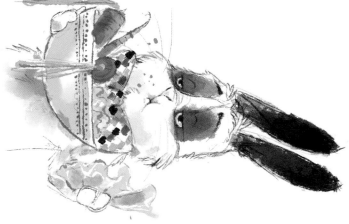

You see, sometimes old, stuffy houses are also lonely.

After breakfast, I hopped to the garden to look at the flowers and say, "Hello, down there!" to the bugs.

Hello, Phil.
Hello, Dennis.

That is when I saw Him. He was a big, fluffy bunny with the floppiest floppy ears and the bushiest bushy tail. He was bunny-beautiful.

I was standing still. But being near him made me feel like my heart was still **hopping**.

"My name is Marlon," I said. "But my family calls me BOTUS. It's short for 'Bunny of the United States.' It's a long story."

"My name is Wesley, and my family calls me Wesley," said Wesley.

Wesley and I hopped together all around the garden.
We hopped over daisies. We hopped over tiny carrots
that weren't ready to grow up and be lunches yet.

We hopped over Phil and Dennis.

Once we had hopped through every part of the garden, we didn't want to stop hopping. So, we hopped right inside the old, stuffy house.

We hopped up and down the creaky stairs and made beautiful, creaky stair-music together.

We hopped through the kitchen and maybe left a few bunny prints.

We hopped through Very Boring Meetings with Very Boring People.

VICE-PRESIDENT

It was a very good hop. It was the Best Hop. And I realized something: when I hopped with Wesley, my old, stuffy house didn't feel lonely anymore.

At the end of our hop, I said, "Wesley, I don't want to hop without you ever again."

And Wesley said, "That's funny, because I never want to hop without you, Marlon Bundo, ever again."

And we both said, "We will get married and hop together Forever."

"Hello, everyone!" we said to all the animals in the garden.

"Hello, Phil and Dennis the bugs, and Pumpernickel who is a badger, and Scooter who is a turtle, and Dill Prickle who is a hedgehog, and Mr. Paws who is a very good dog. Hello, all of you! We are getting married so we can hop together Forever."

"Hooray!" said Phil and Dennis the bugs, and Pumpernickel who is a badger, and Scooter who is a turtle, and Dill Prickle who is a hedgehog, and Mr. Paws who is a very good dog.

"Hooray!" said all of our friends.

Because that is what friends say.

We looked around and saw that the scary voice was coming from The Stink Bug.

Let me tell you a little bit about The Stink Bug. The Stink Bug was In Charge. He was Important. None of the other animals could quite work out why he was In Charge or how he was Important, but he was. And that meant he made the rules. That meant all the animals listened to him even though he was—and this is true—very stinky.

"Boy Bunnies Don't Marry Boy Bunnies!" said The Stink Bug.
"Boy Bunnies Have to Marry Girl Bunnies."

"But this is the Bunny I Love," said Wesley.

"And this is the Bunny I Love," said me, Marlon Bundo.
Just being next to Wesley made me a little braver.

"Too Bad," said The Stink Bug.

"I Am the Stinkiest and I Am Important. I Am the Stinkiest and I Am In Charge. Boy Bunnies Marry Girl Bunnies. Girl Bunnies Marry Boy Bunnies. This Is the Way It Has Always Been. You. Are. Different. And Different Is Bad."

The other animals whispered nervously among themselves.

Pumpernickel, who is a badger, came forward.

"I am different, too," he said. "I eat my sandwiches crust-first."

"I am different, too," said Dill Prickle who is a hedgehog.
"I read the ends of books before I read the beginnings,
just to make sure they're not too sad for me."

OLD YELLER

"I am different, too," said Mr. Paws who is a very good dog.

"Sometimes I sniff butts and I don't know why."

"Everyone is different. And different is *not* bad," said Scooter who is a turtle. "Different is Special."

"Wait!" said Mr. Paws who is a very good dog and also a very *smart* dog. "Wait a minute! We get to decide who is In Charge. We get to decide who is Important. We can vote!"

And on this Very Special Day, all the animals voted on who they wanted to have In Charge.

They chose . . .

...NOT The Stink Bug.

"Hooray!" said me, Marlon Bundo.

"Hooray!" said Wesley.

"Hooray!" said all of our friends. Because that is what friends say.

"NO!" boomed The Stink Bug.
"Boy Bunnies Can't Marry Boy Bunn—"

"YOU ARE NOT
IN CHARGE!"

So, Wesley and I got married. We had two handsome grooms-otters named Muffins and Cubby, and a flower-mouse named Hiccup.

We ate and drank and danced "The Hokey Pokey."

(Dill Prickle was especially good.)

And the ceremony was performed by a cat named Pajama...

...who brought her wife as her date.

After we ate and drank and danced,
we went home.

Together.

"We have to get some sleep, Marlon. Tomorrow we leave on our Bunnymoon."

Because it doesn't matter if you love a girl bunny or a boy bunny, or eat your sandwich backward or forward.

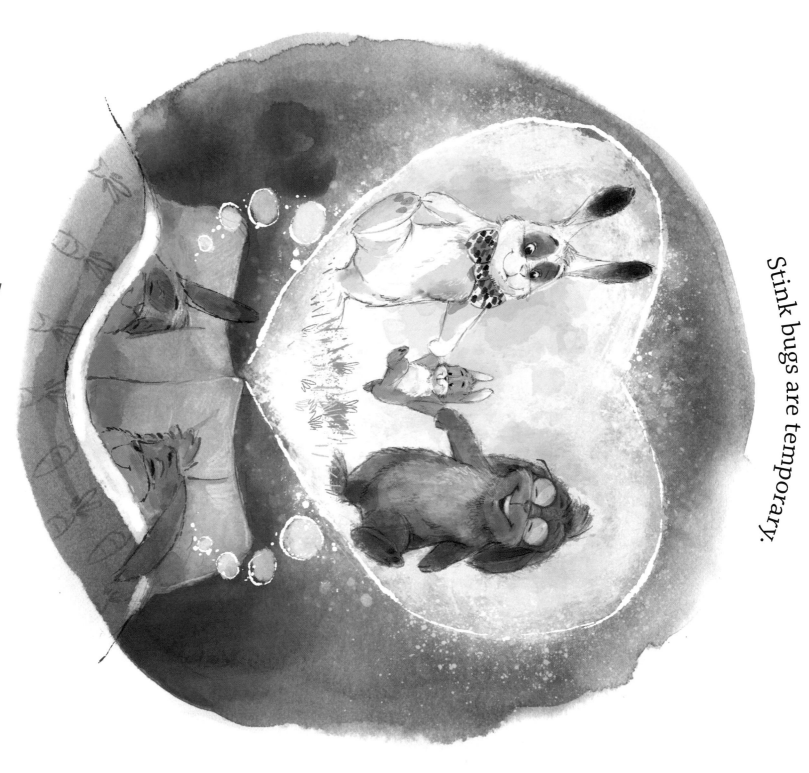

Love is Forever.

Stink bugs are temporary.

For every bunny who has ever felt different.

Copyright © 2018 by Partially Important Productions, LLC

All rights reserved, including the right to reproduce this book or portions thereof in any form whatsoever.

Library of Congress Cataloging-in-Publication Data is available.

ISBN: 978-1-4521-7380-1

Manufactured in the United States of America

Designed by Andrea Miller

10 9 8 7 6

Chronicle Books LLC
680 Second Street
San Francisco, CA 94107
www.chroniclebooks.com

Chronicle books and gifts are available at special quantity discounts to corporations, professional associations, literacy programs, and other organizations. For details and discount information, please contact our premiums department at corporatesales@chroniclebooks.com or at 1-800-759-0190.

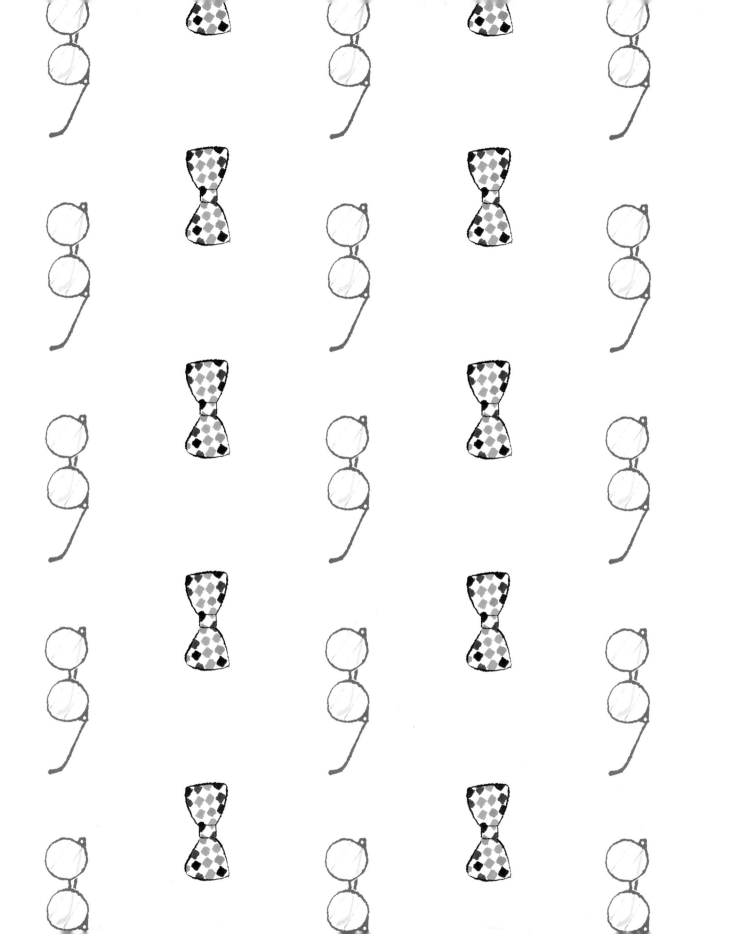